birthday
imagination

Happy birthday, Puffin!

Did you know that in 1940 the very first Puffin story book (about a man with broomstick arms called Worzel Gummidge) was published? That's 70 years ago! Since then the little Puffin logo has become one of the most recognized book brands in the world and Puffin has established its place in the hearts of millions.

And in 2010 we are celebrating 70 spectacular years of Puffin and its books! Pocket Money Puffins is a brand-new collection from your favourite authors at a pocket-money price – in a perfect pocket size. We hope you enjoy these exciting stories and we hope you'll join us in celebrating the very best books for children. We may be 70 years old (sounds ancient, doesn't it?) but Puffin has never been so lively and fun.

There really IS a Puffin book for everyone
– discover yours today.

Charlie Higson is a well-known writer of screenplays and novels, and is the author of the phenomenally successful Young Bond series. He is also a performer and co-creator of *The Fast Show* and *Bellamy's People*.

Books by Charlie Higson

Young Bond:

SILVERFIN

BLOOD FEVER

DOUBLE OR DIE

HURRICANE GOLD

BY ROYAL COMMAND

SILVERFIN: THE GRAPHIC NOVEL

DANGER SOCIETY: THE YOUNG BOND DOSSIER

THE ENEMY

CHARLIE HIGSON

MONSTROSO

PUFFIN

PUFFIN BOOKS

Published by the Penguin Group
Penguin Books Ltd, 80 Strand, London WC2R ORL, England
Penguin Group (USA) Inc., 375 Hudson Street, New York, New York 10014, USA
Penguin Group (Canada), 90 Eglinton Avenue East, Suite 700, Toronto, Ontario, Canada M4P 2Y3
(a division of Pearson Penguin Canada Inc.)
Penguin Ireland, 25 St Stephen's Green, Dublin 2, Ireland (a division of Penguin Books Ltd)
Penguin Group (Australia), 250 Camberwell Road, Camberwell, Victoria 3124, Australia
(a division of Pearson Australia Group Pty Ltd)
Penguin Books India Pvt Ltd, 11 Community Centre, Panchsheel Park, New Delhi – 110 017, India
Penguin Group (NZ), 67 Apollo Drive, Rosedale, North Shore 0632, New Zealand
(a division of Pearson New Zealand Ltd)
Penguin Books (South Africa) (Pty) Ltd, 24 Sturdee Avenue, Rosebank,
Johannesburg 2196, South Africa

Penguin Books Ltd, Registered Offices: 80 Strand, London WC2R ORL, England

puffinbooks.com

First published 2010
1

Set in Adobe Caslon 13.75/21 pt by Ellipsis Books Limited, Glasgow
Made and printed in England by Clays Ltd, St Ives plc

British Library Cataloguing in Publication Data
A CIP catalogue record for this book is available from the British Library

ISBN: 978-0-141-2845-4

www.greenpenguin.co.uk

For my own children, and all the other children who have ever enjoyed a Puffin book.

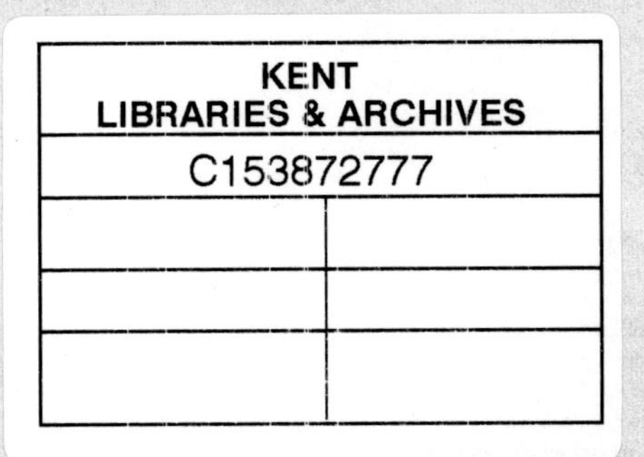

I

'Oscar, we're going away for the night and Grandad will be looking after you.'

'What?'

'We're going away for the night and Grandad will be looking after you.'

'What?'

'I said we're going away for the night and Grandad will be looking after you.'

'What?'

'Grandad will be looking after you on Saturday night, because we're going away . . .'

Oscar was beginning to think that no matter how many times he said 'what', his dad wasn't going to get it. He didn't mean 'what' as in 'What was that you said, darling Papa?' He'd meant 'what' as in 'Please tell me I haven't heard you correctly, you old fool; *please* tell me you are joking – I had plans for this weekend and being stuck with Grandad wasn't one of them.'

Oscar didn't mind too much being left alone with a normal babysitter. He could spend the whole time playing on his computer without being told to stop. But

Oscar's room was used as the spare bedroom, so if guests came to stay he'd be kicked out and have to sleep on a sofa in his dad's office that turned into a bed. (The office didn't turn into a bed, the sofa did. It was a 'sofa bed'. Which meant that it was quite uncomfortable as a sofa and very, very uncomfortable as a bed.)

And if Grandad was in his bedroom Oscar wouldn't be able to get at his computer. Dad kept a laptop in his study but Oscar reckoned it was probably made in the Middle Ages and was the sort of rubbish laptop that King Arthur and His Knights of the Round Table would have used. It was really slow, it kept crashing, the Internet didn't work properly on it and – even worse than that – Oscar wasn't allowed to install any of his games on it.

'You'll slow it down and fill the memory up,' was all Dad ever said if Oscar asked him to put a decent game on it. 'It's not for playing with, it's for work.'

What a stupid thing to say. Everyone knew that computers were for playing with; only idiots used them for work. Dad's computer was nearly as bad as the computers they had at school. There was only one game on the school computers: a really babyish fishing game that Oscar had soon realized was a trick, because it was actually all about learning maths.

So not only would Oscar have to sleep in his dad's horrible office, he would also have to spend half the weekend without his computer.

That wasn't the worst thing, though.

The worst thing was Grandad.

Oscar didn't like his grandad. He was a nuisance. He was always quoting poetry and talking about people Oscar had never heard of and giving Oscar books to read.

'I loved this when I was a boy, Oscar,' he'd say, like that was supposed to make a difference.

At least he didn't smell.

Oscar had heard that some grandads smelled. Oscar's grandad was quite clean and tidy and he didn't have anything mad like a big beard or a wooden leg or a glass eye. It was just that he *would* keep on trying to talk to Oscar. Oscar didn't want to talk to any adults, least of all a prehistoric one like his grandad. The only interesting thing about him was that he'd fought in the Second World War. But he never wanted to talk about it. Oh, no, not Grandad. Grandad loved to drone on about recipes and Charles Dickens and foreign countries and Shakespeare and stupid paintings, but he never wanted to talk about good stuff, like war and battles and killing people and blowing things up.

What was the point of fighting in a war if you never wanted to talk about it?

War was the thing that interested Oscar most in the world. He loved playing at soldiers and playing with soldiers. His room was absolutely filled with toy guns, Action Men and boxes and boxes of little plastic figures. He would happily spend hours drawing pictures of men fighting, the bullets squirting out of machine-guns and zooming away across the paper like swarms of mad bees, aeroplanes raining bombs, little stick men with their heads flying off and big sprays of blood coming out of their necks.

But the best thing was playing war games on his computer.

He could spend whole days doing that. Weeks. Years, if only his mum would let him.

His favourite game was *World of*

Warcraft. It wasn't modern soldiers. It was set in a huge fantasy world of warriors, monsters and magicians, where you could create your own characters and send them out to kill anything that moved.

'Why are you going away?' Oscar asked his mum when he got the chance. 'Where are you going?'

'It's our wedding anniversary and we're going back to stay in the hotel where we had our honeymoon. It'll be romantic.'

Romantic? The more Oscar heard about the hotel, the less he liked the sound of it. It was somewhere in Dorset on a beach with lots of pebbles on it. Why would anyone want to go to a beach that was full of pebbles? Oscar didn't pretend to understand what went through grown-ups' minds, or why they did some of the strange things they did.

'You'll be all right with Grandad, won't you?'

No, of course he wouldn't be all right with Grandad! Grandad was about a million years old and Oscar was just ten. The only good part of Grandad coming to stay was when he left, because he always gave Oscar a sweet. He slipped it into his hand just before he got into the car, like it was a secret between the two of them.

But that wasn't the answer his mum wanted to hear.

'Sure,' he said casually, and then added, 'I'll miss you, though.'

His mum made a wobbly sad face and gave him a big hug.

What Oscar had really meant was that he was going to miss his computer, but he knew that if his mum felt bad about leaving him for the night, she'd spoil him when she got back and maybe let him play extra computer.

'And you'll be all right in Dad's office?'

'Sure. I like it in there.'

Hah! What a terrible lie. It wasn't even a *real* office. Oscar had always pictured an office as a big place full of people wearing suits and working at computers and having important meetings in bright rooms with charts and graphs on the walls. And there would be someone like Sir Alan

Sugar pointing his finger and saying 'You're fired!'

Dad's office was small and dark and gloomy. There was only one window, which looked out on to the wall of the house next door and let in very little light. Mum had tried to brighten things up a bit by hanging some flowery curtains, but they just made things worse. The room had originally been a sort of cupboard with an old boiler in it. The boiler had been taken out and replaced with wonky bookshelves and a tiny desk that was always piled high with paperwork. There was just enough space left for the tatty old sofa bed, a waste-bin and a framed poster for a concert by somebody in a leather jacket called 'Bruce Springsteen'.

'Who's he?' Oscar had asked Dad when he put it up.

'He's The Boss.'

What an idiot Dad was. This wasn't a proper office and by the look of him Bruce Springsteen wasn't a proper boss.

This was going to be an awful weekend.

2

As Oscar helped his dad open the sofa bed out on Saturday morning, Dad said what he always said when Oscar had to sleep in his office.

'You know you're not allowed to touch any of my things, don't you?'

Oscar nodded and looked around the office. Why on earth would he want to touch any of Dad's things? They were *Dad's things*. Dad's things weren't interesting.

But then Oscar noticed something new.

There, sitting in the middle of the desk, was a brand-new laptop. It wasn't shiny black like some laptops, or shiny white like others, or even shiny silver. It was a sort of dull metal colour and quite big.

It was definitely a laptop, though.

Oscar's eyes fell on it like wolves falling on a lamb that has strayed from the flock. Instantly Dad put himself between Oscar and his prey.

'You are absolutely *not* to touch that,' he said. '*Absolutely not*. Do you understand?'

Oscar nodded his head dumbly.

'It's from my work,' Dad went on. 'And

it's got lots of important work things on it. You are absolutely, *absolutely* not to touch it.'

'I won't,' said Oscar. 'I promise.'

But his mind was spinning, his heart racing, his palms sweating. Even as he spoke, he was already working out ways to break his promise without being found out.

Dad occasionally brought things home from work and always made Oscar promise not to touch them. Oscar always promised. It wasn't difficult. Usually it was just books and files and piles of documents in boring grey folders.

His dad worked for the government doing some sort of research. Oscar was never quite sure what, but he boasted to his friends that his dad worked for the army in a secret department where they invented secret weapons. One day Dad had in fact brought home a folder marked 'Top Secret', just like in a James Bond film or something, and Oscar had sneaked into the office and opened the cover. He'd looked at the list of contents. He didn't understand a single word. Then he'd turned to the first page – he didn't understand a single word of that either. He'd flicked through the whole thing. It was all the same.

There weren't even any pictures.

But a computer was different. He understood computers. And what if this was some sort of new government supercomputer? What if it had a lot of Top Secret stuff on it about spies and weapons and new military software? Oscar had heard a lot about new military software. He wasn't sure exactly what it was, except that it was something cool to do with computers in the army and smart bombs.

Oscar liked the idea of smart bombs. He pictured them walking around like extra-clever robots ready to stroll into the enemy base and blow up their generals. What if there were secret controls on the computer for a smart bomb? Or a new game for training soldiers? Oscar had heard that the army had the best warfare simulation games in the world.

Like *World of Warcraft*, only better.

So, while his mouth was saying 'No, I won't', his brain was thinking 'Yes, I will . . .'

3

Dad picked Grandad up after lunch and brought him back to the house. Grandad was quite tall for an old man. He had thin wobbly legs and a big belly. He tottered about like he was drunk. Sometimes he *was* drunk. He had wiry hair that stuck up all over the place, glasses and a big nose.

'How's my favourite grandson?' he said when he came through the door.

He always said that. Oscar would have been quite flattered if Grandad had had any other grandsons. But Oscar was the only one.

Grandad ruffled Oscar's hair.

Oscar made a face.

Grandad laughed.

'How's school?' he said.

Oscar said, 'Good.'

He knew his parents liked it if he said school was good, particularly in front of Grandad. They were always showing off about how well he was doing, even though, as far as Oscar knew, he wasn't doing very well at all. But it seemed to make his parents happy if they all pretended that he was a child genius.

Once Grandad was safely settled in, Mum and Dad were ready to go. Oscar hugged them both and waved them off at the front door.

As Oscar went back inside he realized that he was now alone with Grandad and he might actually have to talk to him. He tried it for a little while but their conversation soon spluttered to a halt and they sat at the kitchen table watching television instead. All the programmes that Oscar wanted to watch he knew Grandad wouldn't like, and all the programmes that Grandad would have liked Oscar didn't want to watch. So they watched a programme that neither of them really wanted to watch and soon got bored.

'Would you like to play a game?' Grandad asked eventually.

Yes, he would like to play a game. On his computer. But he knew that wasn't what Grandad meant. He meant a dreaded board game.

Oscar wondered why the idiots who made 'bored' games couldn't have come up with a better word for their infernal inventions.

'Well, men, we've got these really boring games here. What shall we call them?'

'I know, sir – how about we call them "Exciting games"?'

'Hmmm. I'm not sure. Doesn't sound catchy enough.'

'How about "Thrilling games"?'

'No, might put kids off. I know . . . let's call them "bored games"!'

'Hooray! Great idea, sir. You're a genius!'

Oscar knew he had a long time to get through with Grandad and that if they got off to a good start it might make things easier. So he forced his face into a cheesy smile and said, 'OK, yeah, a board game. That would be fun.'

They went to the cupboard together and looked through the pile of games.

'Monopoly?' said Grandad, pulling out a box that hadn't been touched since the last time he was here.

'Not much fun with only two,' said

Oscar. *Not much fun with any number*, he thought. But he didn't need to tell Grandad that.

Grandad picked out another box. 'What about chess?' he said. 'That's a marvellous game.'

Oscar clamped his mouth shut in an attempt not to scream in terror. Grandad was always trying to teach Oscar the rules of chess. Oscar had struggled and struggled and struggled to understand the blasted rules but he still hadn't the faintest idea how any of the pieces moved, where they moved, or why they would bother moving there in the first place.

He had even tried to think of the pieces as soldiers – it was supposed to be some sort of war game after all, wasn't it? – but it didn't help. Mum had bought him a special set in which the pieces were all knights but all Oscar wanted to do was pick them up and bash them into each other with bloodthirsty cries, not move them ploddingly around the board saying silly things like 'rook to bishop's four' and 'checkmate'. What kind of a war was ever won by someone moving a little piece of knobbly wood on to a square and saying 'checkmate'? Who would ever say that in a battle?

No. You'd say 'Die, you fiend, die!' or 'Ha, ha! Feel my blade in your guts, you ugly swine!'

And what kind of a war ended by

both sides shaking hands and saying 'well played'? It would be much more fun to smash your opponent's pieces to smithereens, burn all their buildings and execute their prawns with a samurai sword.

These were the things he wanted to say to Grandad. Instead he said he was a bit tired after a hard week at school and didn't think his brain could cope with chess.

'Fair point,' said Grandad. 'Not sure my poor old brain could cope very well either. How about a game of cards instead?'

'OK,' agreed Oscar. He had to admit he did sometimes like playing cards, and the two of them spent a reasonably happy time playing rummy. Grandad might have claimed that his brain was tired but it seemed to be working all right and he won nearly as many games as Oscar.

In the end, though, Oscar came out on top.

'Ha!' he said, punching the air. 'Pwned!'

'I beg your pardon?' said Grandad.

'Pwned,' said Oscar. 'I pwned you. P-W-N-E-D, pronounced *poned*.'

'What does that mean?'

'It's like saying I owned you, only a hundred times worse.'

'What do you mean – *owned* me?'

'Beat you! Slaughtered you! Totally wiped you out and ground you into the dirt. Pwned!'

Having played cards for a good half an

hour, Oscar reckoned he'd earned the right to watch some proper TV and they went through to the living room. Oscar put on *SpongeBob SquarePants*. He tried to explain to Grandad what was going on and who the characters were, and Grandad pretended that he was following it but he had that look on his face that Oscar thought he must have on his own face whenever Grandad tried to teach him about chess.

Well, thought Oscar, *we all like different things*. Grandparents like chess and kids like cartoons. Maybe his own grandchildren would like something that he didn't understand. Like, he didn't know, perhaps a game called Bunting-Bonting or a TV programme called *Squiddddink*, or a new type of toy called a Foffo.

As he sat there watching TV he couldn't help thinking about the computer upstairs in Dad's office. Try as he might, he just couldn't get it out of his mind. He pictured it sitting there with all its secrets inside. Waiting for him. Poor lonely computer.

'I think I might like an early night tonight,' he said at last, and Grandad said that would be fine and perhaps he'd turn in early himself.

Good, thought Oscar. Once Grandad was safely out of the way, he could get out of bed and sneak a peek at that computer. That was all. Just a peek. A teeny-tiny peek. Out of the corner of his eye . . .

Where was the harm in that?

They had a supper of sausages and beans and Grandad put him to bed at half past eight. He read a bit from Oscar's favourite *Mister Gum* book. Oscar laughed a lot and Grandad did too. It was quite nice really.

Then Grandad gave him a prickly kiss and left him alone.

Oscar lay there, staring at the laptop on the desk and waiting for Grandad to go to bed. Oh, that laptop was so tempting in its dull grey metal casing. Like an unopened box of chocolates.

Grandad bumbled about a bit down in the kitchen. Then he came plodding up the stairs, huffing and puffing.

PLOD HUFF PLOD PUFF PUFF HUFF PLOD PLOD HUFF . . .

Then CREAK went the bathroom door.

The sounds of water and plumbing and tooth-cleaning came from the bathroom, finishing off with a big KERSPLOOSH as the loo flushed.

CREAK went the door again.

PLOD PLOD PLOD, Grandad plodded along the landing.

CLICK went the landing light.

SQUEAK. That was his bedroom door opening.

KERTHUNK. That was the door shutting.

Now Oscar could hear Grandad shuffling about through the wall. SHUFFLE

SHUFFLE SHUFFLE. When was he going to go to bed?

CLUNK. He'd come out of the bedroom.

CLICK. The landing light was back on.

CREAK went the bathroom door.

KERSPLOOSH went the loo.

CREAK PLOD CLICK SQUEAK KERTHUNK.

Grandad was back in his room.

SHUFFLE SHUFFLE SHUFFLE.

Silence.

Oscar held his breath.

CLUNK CLICK. Oh no! Grandad was up again and on his way back to the bathroom.

How many times did a person need to go to the loo in one night? Was he never actually going to go to sleep?

CREAK PLOD CLICK KER-THUNK SHUFFLE SHUFFLE SHUFFLE.

Silence . . .

More silence . . .

ZZZZZZZZZZZZZ (Snoring).

Hurray!

4

Oscar climbed out of bed. He knew he shouldn't touch the computer. He'd promised Dad. He knew it was very special and important for Dad's work. He knew it was blah-di-blah-di-blah . . .

It was a computer. A COMPUTER! And Oscar LOVED computers.

Before he even knew what he was doing, he found himself lifting open the lid and pressing the power switch. In a few moments the screen lit up and the computer played the little tune that all computers play when they come to life.

Oh, sweet melody!

Oh, *loud* melody!

Oscar prayed that Grandad hadn't heard it. He tiptoed over to the wall and pressed his ear to it. Grandad's snores sounded like the engine of a mighty sports car.

Oscar went back over to the desk and peered at the computer screen. It looked exactly like the welcome screen on his own computer. There were various folders and documents and shortcuts he didn't recognize but his fingers danced across the keys and waggled the little control stick and soon he was searching through the documents for anything that might be important and secret.

He couldn't find anything interesting. Not a sausage. Not even a chipolata. Perhaps the really juicy stuff was hidden away so that hackers couldn't find it. Maybe Oscar would have to break secret codes to get at it?

He yawned. What a dope he'd been. There was nothing secret on here.

It was ridiculous really, to think that this computer might be in any way special.

Even the games on it would probably all be rubbish.

It was worth a look, though . . .

He found the games folder and opened it. He scrolled down the list.

Just as he'd thought.

All the same boring games you got on any computer.

Solitaire, minesweeper, jacks – there was even a chess game.

A chess game! Oscar groaned. If there was anything more boring than playing real chess, it would be playing chess against a computer. What a complete waste of time.

He closed the folder.

And then he spotted something.

His eyes went wide, his heart started knocking against his ribs.

There on the desktop was the image of

a clenched fist with the words PROJECT X written across it in red.

It was a shortcut to a program . . .

Why hadn't Oscar noticed it before? How could he have missed it? His head went all fizzy. His hair was tingling. Like when there was a scary bit in a film. He was sure the icon hadn't been there before. Had it somehow magically appeared?

Don't be stupid.

He must have triggered some secret software on the laptop that had made the icon pop up.

Well, now that it *had* popped up, there was only one thing to do with it . . .

Click on it.

That was what icons were for . . .

PROJECT X.

What could it be? Oscar nervously moved the pointer over it, afraid to click.

He tried to swallow but his mouth was too dry.

Come on, Oscar, don't be a wimp!

He took a deep breath and clicked.

For a moment nothing happened.

Then the screen went black.

What had he done?

After a long and agonizing wait, and just as Oscar was beginning to think he must have killed the computer, the screen started to glow with a strange green light and a throbbing sound came from the speakers. The sound seemed to fill the room. Oscar had no idea how the tiny speakers in the laptop could make such a sound.

But then, this was no ordinary computer.

Two words appeared on the screen.

ENTER USERNAME

Oscar typed in Dad's name. Dad wasn't clever or imaginative enough to come up with a fancy code-name.

DO YOU WISH TO PROCEED, BRIAN?

Oscar clicked on YES.

DO YOU HAVE SECURITY CLEARANCE, BRIAN?

Again Oscar clicked on YES.

ENTER PASSWORD

Oscar knew the answer to that as well. Dad used the same password for everything and Oscar had found it out ages ago when he'd accidentally on purpose overheard him telling it to Mum. He probably could have worked it out for himself anyway. It was an easy one.

Oscar typed in OSCAR1.

PROCEED, BRIAN

Oscar pressed Enter and with a metallic clang the image of a great steel shutter came on to the screen, slamming shut. It immediately snapped open again to reveal a new interface; designed to look like battle-scarred metal, with panels and slots and buttons all over it. There were loads of instructions and options, the same as when you loaded any game. Oscar began to work his way through them. Some of the instructions he didn't understand, so he just skipped through them, clicking on YES or I ACCEPT.

Screen after screen came up with a CLANG and Oscar kept on typing and clicking, his hands dancing over the keyboard like a crazy concert pianist. He realized his fingers were slippery with sweat. They kept sliding off the keys. He'd have to be careful – he'd have to wipe the keyboard when he finished – just like criminals did in films.

At last he reached the screen that asked him if he wanted to run the program. He clicked YES and it was done.

Another page of boxes appeared and Oscar's greedy eyes quickly scanned the options. There were loads of them, most of which Oscar didn't understand, but there, in the lower right-hand corner, was one he was very familiar with:

CREATE YOUR WARRIOR

Warrior!! Yes!!!

It was his type of game. A war game. Maybe a sort of super special secret government version of *World of Warcraft*.

He clicked the box.

He knew what he was doing now. It was time to go to work.

First he selected the sex of his warrior – male, of course. Then the type of warrior. The options were STEALTH, SABOTAGE, ARTILLERY, STRATEGY, SUPPLIES, INFANTRY.

He thought about this for a moment, then clicked on INFANTRY. He wanted a fighting machine. A big tough monster that could smash his way through the enemy lines, with his bare fists if necessary.

Next there were several different skin types to choose from. He picked Rhino Hide.

COLOURS – he chose a cool-looking purple effect with mottled orange patches.

HAIR – Bald.

EYES – Piggy.

JAWS – Massive. With added tusks. Actually he could only afford one tusk. He had something called a DNA bank. The more bits and pieces he added to his warrior, the more points he used up. This was a shame because he had been planning to give his warrior claws and spiked kneecaps. Never mind. He could always make another character later.

The next set of options was for CHARACTER. There were several choices, with sliders next to them:

AGGRESSION

INTELLIGENCE

OBEDIENCE

COURAGE

To start with, the sliders were all set in the middle – 5 out of 10. With all choices being equal. As Oscar increased the Aggression slider upwards, though, he noticed the other sliders move down towards zero. He would have to carefully balance the different sliders.

Well, Oscar didn't have time to be careful. He slid Aggression and Courage up as far as they would go, and pushed Intelligence down to zero, which left Obedience somewhere in the middle.

Who needed intelligence when you were in the business of crushing skulls? But Oscar didn't want his warrior to disobey orders and go rampaging off on his own, so he reduced Aggression and nudged Obedience up a couple of levels.

That would have to do. He was running out of time. He'd already been tapping away for ages and he hadn't even started playing the game yet. Plus he still had to equip his warrior.

Next stop was the armoury where he had to choose his weapons and pay for them from a limited pile of gold coins.

Once he'd bought The Deadly Axe of Death, The Helmet of Doom and The Chainsaw of Destiny, there wasn't much gold left to buy anything else. He quickly paid for a cheap leather breastplate (it was bright pink, which was probably why it was so cheap) and some cool-looking shin-guards before he clicked his way to the quartermaster's stores.

A backpack to keep his items in came as standard, and on top of that Oscar bought some food, a shovel, some magic spells chosen at random from a very long and complicated list, and finally some sunblock. Just in case.

There was just one last thing to do.

NAME YOUR CHARACTER

Oscar typed MONSTROSO THE BLOOD FEASTER.

At least, that was what he *meant* to type, but in his hurry he hit a wrong key and clicked ENTER before he realized his mistake.

That was how his warrior came to be called Monstroso the Bloob Feaster.

5

At last Oscar had reached the final screen. It was plastered with warnings. ARE YOU QUITE SURE BLAH BLAH BLAH . . .? HAVE YOU CHECKED BLAH BLAH BLAH . . .? DO YOU ACCEPT BLAH BLAH BLAH . . .?

'Yes, yes, yes,' Oscar grumbled, 'just *do* it.'

CLICK . . .

The screen went black again, the computer stopped whirring, the throbbing sound died away and . . .

Nothing happened.

'Oh, what?' Oscar tried not to lose his temper. He hated it when you spent hours loading a game and setting it up and tweaking it and then it froze or wouldn't run properly without loads of upgrades and plug-ins.

Useless blimming computer.

He waggled the tiny control stick, he pressed Return over and over again, he tapped random keys on the keyboard – but nothing happened, the screen was blank, the computer was dead, his dreams were dashed.

Oscar groaned, fighting back tears. He was tired, it was late and he'd just wasted over an hour of his precious young life.

He beat his fists on the desk – not too hard in case it woke Grandad. Then he swore, jabbed the power off, and closed the screen.

He slid down from the chair and turned round.

And nearly died of fright.

There, standing behind him, was a bald, seven-foot-tall, purple and orange monster wearing pink armour. He had a pack on his broad back with a helmet dangling from it and an axe slung across one shoulder. Gripped in his massive hands was a golden chainsaw with the words

DEATH TO WIMPS painted on it in what looked like blood.

It was Monstroso.

Oscar looked at Monstroso and Monstroso looked at Oscar.

Oscar gulped. Monstroso blinked.

And then he spoke; with a voice so deep it rattled the pens in the jamjar on Dad's desk.

'What are your orders, General?'

Oh God, there were two of them! A general as well! Oscar glanced nervously around the office. Where was the other one?

And then he realized his mistake. Monstroso thought *he* was a general.

'Er, are you t-talking to me?' he stammered.

'What are your orders, General Brian?'

'Um, er . . . I don't really have any orders . . .'

'Monstroso need orders. Monstroso need fight. Monstroso need *kill*.'

'Couldn't Monstroso just sit down quietly for a moment while the general has a bit of a think?'

'I am Monstroso the Bloob Feaster. I am here to fight, not sit quietly.'

'Not Bloob Feaster, you idiot!' said Oscar. '*Blood* Feaster.'

'Nay, my lord,' growled Monstroso. 'I am a Bloob Feaster! The greatest Bloob Feaster in the kingdom. Show me some bloob that I may feast upon it.'

'I don't have any bloob,' squeaked Oscar.

'Then Monstroso will scour the land searching for fresh bloob!'

'No you will not. And that's an order.'

'Aye, General . . . Are you sure you have no bloob?'

'I'm positive. Now stop going on about it.'

'Aye, aye, sir. Your word is my command.'

'Good. And don't you forget that.'

'Forget what? Monstroso not have good memory.'

CLUNK. SHUFFLE SHUFFLE. CLICK.

Oh no. Grandad had woken up!

'Get down on the floor,' Oscar hissed. 'Make yourself small.'

'Huh? Monstroso not understand.'

'Shut up and get on the floor! That's an order, soldier.'

Monstroso did as he was told, as Oscar quickly ripped down the flowery curtains from the window and threw them over him.

There was a quiet knock at the door, then Grandad's voice.

'Oscar? Are you all right?'

'I'm fine, Grandad.'

'I heard a noise. Are you sure you're all right?'

'I couldn't sleep. I was listening to a story tape. I'm sorry if it was too loud.'

The door opened and there was Grandad's face. He looked very old and tired. His eyes were small and helpless without his glasses. His hair all messed up.

'I'm sorry I woke you,' said Oscar.

'That's all right. I need to use the bathroom anyway.'

'OK.'

Grandad peered at the huge curtain-covered lump in the middle of the room. Trying to remember if it had been there before. He shook his head and smiled at Oscar.

'Well, if you're sure you're all right.'

'I'm fine. Goodnight, Grandad.'

'Goodnight.'

Grandad closed the door, shuffled to the bathroom and after a while Oscar heard the loo flush. Then Grandad shuffled back to his room and after a few minutes started snoring again.

The shape on the floor rose up to form a hulking, curtain-covered blob.

'Monstroso kill old man?' said the warrior, his deep gruff voice muffled by the flowery material.

'No, Monstroso not kill anyone,' said Oscar, pulling the curtains off him. 'Monstroso needs to get back inside the computer.'

'Monstroso not understand. What is "computer"?'

'The cause of all our problems.' Oscar pointed to the laptop and Monstroso peered at it.

'You want Monstroso smash?'

'No.'

'Monstroso getting bored. If Monstroso not smash something soon, Monstroso go stark raving bonkers. Monstroso live only to fight. Crunch! Kill! Destroy! What you want Monstroso destroy, my general?'

'I don't want you to destroy anything,' Oscar groaned.

'Please, General Brian.'

'Don't call me that,' Oscar snapped.

'What you want Monstroso call you?'

'Oscar. General Oscar.'

'Aye, aye, Oscar-General-Oscar.'

Monstroso saluted and fired up his chainsaw.

'What are you doing?' Oscar shrieked. 'Turn that off!'

Monstroso made a grumpy face and shut the chainsaw's engine down. Oscar took the chainsaw off him and put it on a shelf.

'Just stand to attention and do nothing until further orders.'

'Aye aye, sir!'

Oscar tugged at his hair, trying to think. 'This is all that stupid computer's fault,' he moaned.

'Monstroso smash computer!'

Oscar shouted 'NO', but it was too late. Monstroso brought the Deadly Axe of Death crashing down on to the laptop, chopping computer – and desk – in half.

'Stop! That's an order!'

He was beginning to wish he'd given Monstroso a few more brains.

'Monstroso not want stop. Monstroso happy now. Monstroso smash something. Monstroso like smashing things.'

'Monstroso must do what he is told.'

'Monstroso live only to smash and kill and feast on bloob!'

'You can't just spend your life smashing things up and killing things. There must be something else you like doing.'

'Monstroso like to play Bunting-Bonting. Monstroso captain of Bloob Feaster first eleven. Win Armageddon world cup. Celebrated by cutting off heads of losing team.' The memory made Monstroso smile and run a warty thumb along the sharp edge of his axe.

'Monstroso must obey orders,' said Oscar.

Monstroso squinted at Oscar with a shifty look in his piggy eyes. His tiny brain was spinning in his bony head. Working out how much he could get away with. Oscar wished he'd given Monstroso the full level 10 obedience. If he didn't keep the warrior happy, he might mutiny. If only Oscar had given him more obedience and less aggression.

And more brains.

A lot more brains.

Well, it was too late to change that now. In fact, it was too late to change anything – the laptop was smashed to smithereens.

Oscar jumped as there came another knock on the door. Grandad must have woken up again.

'Oscar, I heard a thump.'

'Sorry, Grandad. I was just getting up for a glass of water and I bumped into the desk in the dark.'

'Oh, OK.'

Monstroso leaned over, licking his lips, and whispered in Oscar's ear.

'Monstroso chop old man in half like computer.'

'No,' hissed Oscar.

But they *would* have to do something with Grandad while Oscar figured a way out of this horrible mess. He waited until he could hear the old man snoring again and sat down to talk to Monstroso. It wasn't easy – for a start, Monstroso smelled something rotten and he kept farting and belching. Secondly, he couldn't sit still for two seconds. Thirdly, he was dribbling on to the carpet. Fourthly, . . .

Oscar stopped counting at four, or he'd be here all night.

'What spells do you have in your back-pack?' he asked the stupid lump when they'd given up on all other ideas (they'd already discussed tying Grandad up, knocking him out and locking him in the attic).

'Monstroso not need magic. Only axe and chainsaw.'

'Yes, all right,' said Oscar. 'But *I* need

some magic. OK? And I know you've got some potions in your backpack, because I put them in there earlier. I'm just not sure what I bought and what any of it does. Do you have anything like a sleeping potion? Or something to slow an enemy down without actually hurting them?'

'Hmm . . . I have Chestnut Surprise.'

'What does that do?'

'It turn enemy into a tree.'

'That might work, I suppose,' said Oscar, who was desperate enough to try anything. 'How long does it last?'

'One hundred and twenty-seven years.'

'That's no good,' said Oscar. 'Mum and Dad will be back tomorrow. I'm not sure how I would explain the fact that Grandad had disappeared and there was a dirty great chestnut tree growing in my bedroom. Anything else?'

'Befuddle.'

'How does that work?'

'Scramble brain, turn Grandad doolally. Grandad not be actual tree, just *think* he is tree.'

'No, that sounds like it might be dangerous.'

'Oh! Monstroso have vial of Night-time Freezarium.'

Oscar vaguely remembered picking the Freezarium out from a row of similar-sounding magic potions.

'How does that work?'

'It stop time and freeze enemy until break of day.'

'Perfect! Now show me how to use it.'

6

Ten minutes later Oscar was creeping down the landing towards where Grandad's rasping snores were coming out of his bedroom. He was carrying a thin glass bottle of blue liquid. When he got to the bedroom door, he pushed it open a crack. Grandad's snoring was almost deafening.

Then the snoring stopped and Oscar heard Grandad stirring in his bed. He sat up and blinked at the light that was coming in at the door. He reached for his glasses and Oscar quickly threw the bottle into the room. There was a smash and a tinkle and Oscar slammed the door. He counted to ten like he'd been told and then tried to open the door again.

It wouldn't budge. There was something blocking it from the other side.

He shoved and grunted and grunted and shoved but couldn't get the door to shift even half an inch. The problem was solved by Monstroso who came up behind him, grabbed the door and ripped it off its hinges.

Oscar was going to say something when his attention was caught by the doorway.

Although it should have now been empty, it was still blocked. By a solid wall of blue jelly. Jelly filled his room. And there, encased in the middle of it all, was Grandad, frozen at the moment of sitting up in bed and reaching for his glasses with a startled look on his face.

Oscar turned to Monstroso.

'Will he be all right?'

'Him OK,' said Monstroso. 'Him not remember a thing.'

'Good,' said Oscar. 'Now we've got to fix this door, then we've got to fix the desk, then we've got to fix the computer and then we've got to send you back to where you came from.'

'Monstroso not go back. Monstroso like

it here. Monstroso having fun. Maybe just smash a few more things and do some nice killing.'

'No killing.'

'Not even just a little bit?'

'No. We don't need to smash things – we need to fix things.'

'Monstroso have idea.'

'Is it a good idea?'

'It best I can manage. Monstroso not good with ideas. Monstroso mainly just like to kill and smash and feast on bloob.'

'Blood! Feast on *blood*!'

'Monstroso like to feast on blood too. But bloob better. More vitamins.'

'All right, all right. So what's your big idea?'

'Monstroso have magic that might fix computer.'

'What is it?'

'Super goo.'

'Super goo?'

'Aye. Super goo fix anything. Broken leg, broken sword . . .'

'Broken computer?'

'Super goo fix anything! Just be careful not to get it on hands or it stick fingers together.'

'Brilliant! Let's try it.'

The super goo was in another glass bottle. It was a thick, clear liquid that smelled of hamsters. Monstroso explained that Oscar would only need to use one drop, and Oscar figured it would be safest to try it on the desk first.

They shoved the two halves of the desk roughly next to each other and Oscar dripped two drops of super goo on to the join. Then, before his eyes, the liquid started to boil and bubble and expand. Lumps seemed to be forming in it, no, not lumps, tiny people. They were emerging from the bubbling goo like ants from a hole in the ground. Hundreds of them, almost too small to see, moving so fast that Oscar felt like he was watching some crazy speeded-up film. Some had tools – hammers and axes, saws and mallets – others used long ropes to pull stacks of tiny planks on log rollers, one group started building scaffolding, some more set up a tiny blacksmith shop, complete with minuscule fires and red-hot metal. Oscar heard the sound of tiny trumpets and noticed that some of the workforce were cracking whips like slave drivers. And still they kept coming, swarming out of the bubbling goo in all directions. There were thousands of them now, an army of tireless slaves. They set to work on the desk, sawing, hammering, chopping, singing work songs, filling gaps with what looked like cement, while the whips cracked and the trumpets tooted and orders were shouted. It took them only a couple of minutes to knit the splintered wood back together. Then more trumpets sounded and more orders were yelled and the tiny,

tiny men started to dissolve into the desk, filling any last small holes and scratches until finally the desk looked as good as new.

Oscar looked at the bottle of goo.

'This stuff is sick,' he said. 'Let's see if it works on the computer.'

He grabbed the ruined computer and put the two halves next to each other on the desktop.

He dripped on just a single drop this time and almost immediately there came a trumpet call and a fresh army of tiny slaves poured out over the mangled plastic and metal of the laptop, working feverishly to put it back together.

They were even faster this time and

Oscar couldn't keep up with the manic progress. One minute there was a mangled heap of junk sitting there, and the next there was a nice, solid laptop looking as good as new.

Oscar cheered and carefully replaced the stopper in the bottle of precious liquid before inspecting the computer.

'It looks all right,' he said, switching on the power. 'But the question *is* – will it work properly?'

As before, the laptop played its little song and lit up – and there on the desktop was the icon for PROJECT X. Oscar clicked on it.

That was when things started to really go wrong.

The computer made a horrible grinding sound, then whirred and clicked and whirred some more, like a wheezy kid with asthma.

'What's it doing?'

'You want Monstroso kill it again?'

'No!'

Instead of opening the program, the computer spluttered to a halt and froze. Oscar swore and was just about to try hitting some buttons when the screen did something weird. It started to expand, growing taller and wider, like a black hole opening up in the middle of the room.

No, not a black hole – a *doorway*.

'Portal is open,' Monstroso announced.

'Then back you go,' said Oscar.

Monstroso looked hurt. Like a big kid. He hung his head and shuffled his feet.

'Monstroso not go. Monstroso stay. Monstroso like Oscar-General-Oscar.'

'Back you go. That's an order!' said Oscar, but then he stopped. He had heard something. Heavy footsteps. Far off, but growing closer. Like an elephant approaching. An elephant wearing iron boots.

'What's that?' he asked, turning to Monstroso.

'This not good,' said Monstroso.

'I had a feeling you were going to say that.'

A bright yellow circle appeared in the middle of the portal – it was spinning and it grew quickly bigger . . .

And bigger and bigger and . . .

'Duck!' yelled Monstroso, pulling Oscar to the floor.

A ball of fire flew out of the portal and hit Dad's framed Bruce Springsteen poster bang in the middle. That was the end of the poster. That was the end of the wall behind it as well. The fireball had melted a big round hole in it.

Now what?

Oscar's silent question was answered almost immediately as a huge figure blundered out of the portal and looked around the office.

It was another warrior. He must have been about eight foot tall, with yellow skin and blood-red armour. He carried a huge sword in one hand and a flamethrower in the other. Oscar wouldn't have thought it possible, but this warrior was uglier, meaner and even more stupid-looking than Monstroso. What's more, he had a pair of spiked kneecaps just like the ones Oscar had wanted to get for Monstroso.

'What the hell is it?' said Oscar.

'It's The Rofl!' said Monstroso.

'The Rofl?'

'The Rofl from the plains of Noob!'

The Rofl spotted the two of them, roared and raised its flamethrower.

Monstroso let out a roar of his own, sprang up and swiped at The Rofl with his axe before he could fire again. The Rofl jumped back and Monstroso's axe missed him completely and instead trashed an entire shelf of books. Shredded pages fluttered in the air like snow.

Monstroso and The Rofl yelled at each other and set to, axe clashing against sword, sword clashing against bookcase, bookcase falling on desk, axe smashing light, sword smashing window, axe clashing against sword again, flamethrower whacking Monstroso around head, Monstroso falling through hole in wall.

CLASH THUMP CRASH CLANG TINKLE CLASH WHACK THUD GULP.

(The gulp at the end was Oscar gulping.)

The Rofl grinned, showing a mouth full of rotten green teeth. Once again he raised his flamethrower and aimed it at Oscar.

Oscar opened his mouth to scream and the next thing he knew he was flying backwards through the air. Monstroso had stuck his hand back through the hole in the wall and grabbed him. He hauled him out of the room and on to the landing as a ball of flame whizzed past their heads and set fire to the banisters.

Monstroso didn't wait for the next shot. He raced down the stairs with Oscar tucked under his arm.

They dashed into the kitchen and hid behind the fridge.

'Can you kill it?' Oscar panted.

'Him stronger. Him have better weapon.'

Even as Monstroso said it, the kitchen door exploded into flames and then shattered as The Rofl barged in, howling. Monstroso was up and at him with his axe, but it was a very one-sided fight. The Rofl seemed to be playing with him, knocking him off his feet and then waiting for him to get up before swatting him down again.

KERRRUNCH . . . That was the kitchen table being flattened.

GNRRRRR THUD . . . That was The Rofl picking up the fridge and dropping it on Monstroso.

FRAWWWWWW SKREEE SLAM PING . . . That was The Rofl picking Monstroso up by one foot and throwing him against the oven. (The ping was the oven timer chiming.)

KABOOOM! That was the oven exploding.

CRACK CLATTER CLATTER CLATTER . . . That was Monstroso's head being rammed into the food cupboard and all the tins falling out.

Oscar cowered in the corner and watched as the kitchen was steadily smashed to pieces.

And then he remembered the magic potions.

7

Oscar waited for Monstroso to come near and then jumped on to his back. As Monstroso blundered about the room, dodging blows and destroying first the TV, then the tumble-drier, Oscar wrestled the backpack open and felt around inside it.

He grabbed a handful of the bottles and jumped down just as The Rofl caught Monstroso with a side-swipe that sent him tumbling into the dishwasher, which crumpled and started to squirt out a fountain of hot water.

Oscar scurried away from the fight and looked at the bottles of magic potion. He recognized one as the super goo and was soon up and darting around the kitchen, madly dripping drops of magic liquid on to all the things that the two monsters had broken in their fight. TOOT TOOT went the tiny trumpets, CRACK went the whips, and soon the whole kitchen was swarming with an infestation of nano-slaves, singing their work songs, swinging their hammers, slinging their thread-like ropes. A brand-new fridge sprang up only to be flattened again. The cooker was quickly rebuilt, but was sliced in half once more by The Rofl's gigantic sword. A heap of broken crockery was neatly stacked into a gleaming pile of plates, only to be picked up and smashed over Monstroso's head.

This was no good. No good at all. If Oscar couldn't stop the fight somehow it was a complete waste of time fixing anything. He would be forever mending stuff only to see it broken again. And he felt sorry for the little men; all their work was in vain.

Oscar looked at the other bottles he'd rescued.

Maybe one of them would be some use?

Nope, nope, no, no . . .

Aha! That might do the trick!

The only problem would be getting close to The Rofl without being flattened like the fridge, sliced in half like the cooker or picked up and smashed over Monstroso's head like the pile of plates.

He would have to hurry, though. Monstroso was on his last legs, staggering about, barely able to lift his big arms to defend himself from the blows that The Rofl was raining down on him.

Oscar held on to the bottle tightly and crept out of his hiding-place, using a saucepan lid as a shield.

For the moment The Rofl was distracted. Too busy kneeling down and pummelling Monstroso's head through the floorboards to notice Oscar edging closer.

Oscar took a deep breath and drew back his arm, ready to throw the bottle. If only The Rofl would raise its head to make a better target.

Oscar had seen lots of action films; he knew just what to do.

'Come and get it, you big ugly lump!'

Oscar immediately realized that shouting at The Rofl had been a big mistake.

The Rofl looked up, and did the following – though not necessarily in this order (it was hard to tell, it all happened so fast) – saw Oscar, grinned, let go of Monstroso, grabbed Oscar in one giant yellow fist, squeezed hard and stood up.

Oscar squirmed and twisted, but he was held fast, his arms pinned to his sides.

Then he shouted 'HELP!' It wasn't the most original thing to shout, but it seemed like the right thing to do at the time.

Monstroso raised his battered head and squinted up at Oscar.

'My general . . .' he muttered – and bit The Rofl's big toe.

The Rofl squealed and stomped on Monstroso, forgetting about Oscar for a moment.

It was all Oscar needed. The Rofl's grip

loosened just enough for him to wriggle his hand free and hurl the bottle of potion at the warrior's head.

There was a pop, a flash, a cloud of foul-smelling green smoke, a loud crunchy crackling sound, then a deafening roar like a waterfall as Oscar found himself zooming upwards at a dizzy rate, as if he was on a fairground ride. A very dangerous fair-ground ride. Dust and bricks and bits of wood fell past him as . . .

CRASH . . . he went through the kitchen ceiling . . .

WHOOSH . . . he whizzed up past the blazing banisters . . .

CRUNCH . . . he went through the next ceiling . . .

AIEEEEE . . . he went through the attic . . .

and . . .

SMASH . . . out through the roof . . .

Roof tiles and cobwebs and tufts of loft insulation were swirling through the air all around him as still he zoomed upwards.

And then he stopped, dangling in the night sky several metres above the roof-tops. It was dark and chilly up here.

Oscar looked around.

A canopy of leaves spread above his head, blotting out the stars. The Rofl's hand had become a gnarled and twisted branch. His body the trunk of a mighty tree.

The Chestnut Surprise potion had certainly surprised *this* monster.

Oscar looked down.

The towering chestnut tree that had once been The Rofl stuck up through a jagged black hole in the roof of Oscar's house.

This was going to be really hard to explain to Mum and Dad.

8

Lights were coming on in the houses all around. People must have been woken up by the sound of the tree breaking through the roof and wondered what on earth it was.

Oscar had to get down from here. But he was held fast. The branch around his waist was as thick as . . . well, as thick as The Rofl's arm.

Now what? Would he have to wait for

the fire brigade to come and cut him free?

No. He had to sort out this whole mess before he got into more trouble than any boy had ever been in before.

And besides, if Monstroso saw a bunch of men in helmets approaching Oscar wielding axes he would more than likely attack them with The Chainsaw of Destiny.

Monstroso! There he was, climbing up the tree, a look of concentration on his big stupid face. He reminded Oscar of something. Oh yes. King Kong climbing the skyscraper at the end of the film.

Monstroso struggled up to Oscar's branch, puffing and panting, and then nervously inched along it towards Oscar.

'Monstroso not like heights.'

He got to Oscar, surveyed the situation and snapped the branch as if it was a little twig, then, holding Oscar under one smelly armpit, he climbed all the way back down again. When they got to the upstairs landing Monstroso jumped off, groaned and flopped down against the wall. Oscar thanked him, and started to gabble on about the fight, the words tumbling out of him in a mad rush. 'What about when the fireball dissolved the wall, and when you bit his toe, yeah, and when he whacked you over the head with the plates and, oh yeah, remember when you –'

Oscar stopped. Monstroso wasn't listening. His piggy eyes were bloodshot, his breathing thin and raspy. He was shivering. Pale. Feeble-looking.

'Are you all right?' Oscar asked.

Monstroso slowly shook his head and closed his eyes.

Oscar knelt by his side and slapped his face.

'Monstroso! Wake up!'

Monstroso's eyelids fluttered open and he looked, cross-eyed, at Oscar.

'Monstroso not feel too chipper. Rofl kill Monstroso.'

'No. You'll be OK. You're a big strong monster.'

'Monstroso broken . . .'

'No!' Oscar threw his arms round the big purple body. 'You're not going to die.'

'Nay, my general. Monstroso has feasted on his last bloob. No more games of Bunting-Bonting. Monstroso go to the big battlefield in the sky . . .'

Oscar wiped away a tear. Monstroso was the cause of all his problems. Because of him the house was trashed, a tree grew out of the ruins and his grandad was encased in jelly . . .

Oscar sniffed. Monstroso may have been stupid but he was loyal.

'So long, Oscar-General-Oscar . . . it was pleasure to serve under you . . .'

'No! Wait! I know. The super goo! You said it could fix anything. Could it fix you?'

'Oscar-General-Oscar need goo to fix house . . .'

'No. That's not important. Will it fix *you*?'

'Think so . . . But need lots to mend broken body . . .'

Oscar raced down to the kitchen and searched through the debris until he found the little stash of bottles he'd rescued from Monstroso's pack. He bounded back upstairs with them three steps at a time.

Monstroso looked even worse. He was slumped sideways, hardly breathing at all.

Oscar took one look around at his ruined house. It was a total wreck. The super goo could fix everything. Put it back to how it was. Make everything OK . . .

'Here,' he said, unstopping the bottle

and putting it to Monstroso's lips. 'Drink this.'

He tipped the liquid in. From deep inside Monstroso came the sound of trumpets and whip cracks and work songs. The big monster wobbled and giggled, and smoke came out of his ears. He went cross-eyed. He choked and spluttered, gasped, belched, farted, dribbled, hooted like an owl, squawked like a parrot, whistled like a kettle and then slumped back lifelessly against the wall.

'Monstroso . . .?'

Oscar stared at his new friend with tears in his eyes, hoping against hope that he was all right.

Then a tiny general, no bigger than a grain of rice, appeared in Monstroso's left nostril and saluted Oscar, before dissolving into a pool of snot.

Monstroso's eyes snapped wide open and he sat upright.

'Monstroso good! Monstroso kill!'

He grinned at Oscar and gave him a squeeze that nearly broke Oscar's spine.

'Oscar good friend. Oscar save Monstroso's life! Monstroso serve Oscar till end of time!'

Now it was Oscar's turn to slump against the wall.

'Look at this place,' he said. 'What am I going to say to Mum and Dad?'

Monstroso winked.

'Monstroso have one last bottle of magic,' he said. 'Make everything all right!'

Oscar brightened.

'Good old Monstroso. What's the potion?'

'Summon Skofirax.'

'You're sure it'll help?'

'Help much. Big powerful magic!'

'Come on, then,' said Oscar. 'Let's do it.'

Monstroso picked up one of the bottles and got ready to throw it on to the carpet. At the last moment Oscar grabbed his arm and gave him a stern look. It would be silly to forget just how stupid Monstroso was.

'You're sure this won't be a mistake?'

'Not mistake.'

'It won't be harmful to us in any way?'

'Not harmful. Monstroso never harm Oscar-General-Oscar. Oscar-General-Oscar Monstroso's friend.'

'Fine. Do it then . . .'

Monstroso smashed the bottle. A stinking cloud of pinkish-blueish-brownish-blackish smoke billowed up from the floor, then, slowly, from out of the smoke a creature formed. It was hairless, with a teeny-tiny head on a long neck, very big eyes, buck teeth, short back legs and a fat belly.

It was about fifteen centimetres tall.

It squeaked 'I am Skofirax!', looked at Monstroso and Oscar, blinked, then shrieked and ran full pelt across the floor, making a sort of high-pitched chattering noise that sounded very much like it was shouting, 'No no no no no no no no no no no no . . .'

It ran into the tree trunk, gave another squeak and fell back, stunned. Then it picked itself up, squeaked 'I am Skofirax!' again, gave another startled, wide-eyed look to Monstroso and Oscar, then ran full pelt in the opposite direction before colliding with the wall and falling over again.

'Oh yes,' said Oscar. 'Very useful.'

'Skofirax funny,' said Monstroso. 'Skofirax make Monstroso laugh.'

'And how exactly does that help?'

'It important to laugh now and then.'

'But what's funny?' said Oscar. 'Hmm?

What can I possibly laugh at? First of all I used the computer without permission, even though I promised, then I demolished Dad's office, there's a hole in the wall, his Bruce Springsteen poster's been zapped, Grandad's encased in a block of jelly, the banisters are on fire, the kitchen's in ruins . . . and there's a dirty great chestnut tree poking up through the middle of the house! So will you please tell me what *exactly* is funny?'

'Skofirax funny. Look.'

The Skofirax was pelting about the landing, bumping off the walls like a demented pinball, taking it in turns to shout 'I am Skofirax!' and 'No no no no no no no no no no no no . . .'

Oscar looked at it. He had to admit it was quite comical. He tittered. He snorted.

The Skofirax fell down the stairs, bouncing all the way to the bottom upside down, squeaking 'No!' each time his head hit a new step.

Oscar snorted again, guffawed, and let out a burst of uncontrollable giggles.

Soon the two of them were helpless with laughter as they heard the poor bewildered Skofirax bumping about downstairs.

'The only thing is,' Oscar groaned between sobs of laughter, 'Mum and Dad are going to be home soon . . .'

Through the hole in the roof Oscar could see that the sky was growing pale.

There was the sound of sirens coming nearer.

That would be the police, the fire brigade, ambulances, TV crews . . .

And that was when they heard the voice . . .

9

The portal had shrunk and there was a long bony hand poking out of the laptop screen. It looked impossibly old and wrinkled. A ring circled its outstretched finger. A gold ring with a weird glowing blue and green pattern on it that seemed to be always changing.

The voice was coming from deep inside the blackness. It sounded ancient and wise and scary and far away and close and loud and quiet all at the same time.

'Monstroso!' it was saying. 'Monstroso, Monstroso, Monstroso . . .'

'What is it, master?'

'You disobeyed me, Monstroso! You should not have stepped through the portal.'

'Monstroso sorry . . . but Monstroso smelled fresh bloob!'

'Monstroso has been very, very bad . . .' The finger wagged at him. 'I warned you never to step into the realm of humans. Now I will have to put right what you have done. If the humans ever find out about our realm, it will be the end for us!'

Now the pointing finger swung round and aimed itself at Oscar.

'You! What is your name?'

'O-O-Oscar,' Oscar stammered.

'Well, O-O-Oscar, did you summon Monstroso to your realm?'

'Y-yes, but I didn't mean to . . . I thought it was a game . . .'

'A GAME!' The voice roared like thunder, rattling the room and causing several bricks to fall out of the half-demolished wall. 'Not everything is a game, boy!'

'I know. I'm sorry.'

'Being sorry is not enough. Have you learned your lesson?'

'Y-yes . . . But please, can you help

me? I'm in terrible trouble, and –'

'BE SILENT!'

'Sorry,' mumbled Oscar.

'I suppose,' said the voice, quieter now and more gentle, 'you did show great bravery, and loyalty to Monstroso. You could have saved yourself and you chose to save him. This act of kindness shall be rewarded.'

'Thank you,' said Oscar.

'But first you must carry out the ancient ritual of Hunstanton.'

'Er . . . OK . . .'

The hand slowly withdrew into the screen, only to reappear a short while later with something white dangling from the outstretched finger.

'Put these underpants on your head.'

'OK.' Oscar slipped the underpants over his head (first having a quick look to make sure they were clean).

'Now stand on one leg,' said the voice of doom.

Oscar stood on one leg.

'Now make a face like a frightened beaver.'

Oscar stuck out his top teeth, opened his mouth wide and tried to look scared. He hoped it would look all right, but he hadn't ever seen a frightened beaver so he wasn't sure.

'You look more like a startled ferret,' said the voice.

'It's the best I can do,' said Oscar, wobbling on his one leg.

'Very well. Now say after me . . . I am a poltroon.'

'I am a poltroon.'

Oscar could hear the sirens getting nearer and nearer. How long was this going to take?

'I am a twerp of the highest order . . .'

'I am a twerp of the highest order.'

'A level eighty nitwit . . .'

'A level eighty nitwit.'

'Good,' proclaimed the voice, satisfied, 'then kiss the Ring of Gnir and all will be well again!'

Oscar leaned forward and pressed his lips against the ice-cold surface of the ring . . .

10

'Oscar?'

'Huh?'

'Did you fall asleep in front of the telly?'

'Eh?'

Oscar sat up and rubbed his eyes. He was on the sofa in the living room. He looked at the clock.

Half past four. In the afternoon.

'Are you OK, Oscar, darling?'

It was Mum. Oscar jumped up and gave her the biggest hug of his life.

He let her go.

'Er . . .' He looked around. 'Is everything all right?'

'How do you mean?'

'The house? Grandad? The big tree . . .'

'Everything's fine – why? What tree?'

'Oh . . . nothing . . .'

Dad came in, carrying a suitcase.

'Hello, mate,' he said, and Oscar hugged him too. He'd done more hugging in the last twenty-four hours than in the last five years.

'Oh, Dad,' he said. 'I'm really, really, really, really sorry . . .'

'What for? What's up?'

'I used your computer, your special one from work. I know I said I wouldn't, but I . . .'

Dad laughed.

'Don't worry about it, mate. That computer's nothing special. It's just an old thing they were throwing out at work. To tell you the truth, I brought it home for you. Thought you might find a use for it. I only told you not to touch it because I didn't want you being stuck in front of a screen all weekend. Thanks for owning up, though.'

'But the programs on it . . .'

'There's no programs on it. I got the computer guys at work to wipe the hard drive.'

'What about Project X?'

'Project X? What on earth are you on about? Come on, let's get something to eat, I'm starved. You can tell us all about what you've been up to and then I'll have to get Grandad home.'

11

An hour later Grandad was standing by the front door, ready to go. He looked neat and smart and jolly, rabbiting on about a book on eels that he'd just read.

'Amazing creatures, and we understand so little about them. Every one of them is born in the Sargasso Sea . . .'

Dad was carrying Grandad's battered

old suitcase and trying to get him out of the door and into the car.

Oscar kissed Grandad goodbye. He felt a little awkward and guilty about what he'd done to the poor old man last night, encasing him in jelly and everything, but Grandad didn't seem any the worse for it. In fact, if anything, he seemed a little brighter and livelier. Maybe it had never happened? Maybe it was a dream. There were no signs anywhere of last night's battle. One moment Oscar had been kissing the Ring of Gnir and the next . . . It was twelve hours later and all was well in the world.

As they walked out to the car, Oscar couldn't help smiling. It was a lovely day.

A blue sky and birds twittering in the trees. A normal day. A peaceful day. Oscar had realized one thing: warfare was all very well in a computer game, but it was something very different in real life.

He hurried to catch up with Grandad. He didn't want to miss out on the boiled sweet he always slipped him when he left. Grandad stopped by the car and turned round.

'See you soon, I hope,' said Oscar.

Grandad grinned, showing his gleaming white false teeth, and leaned down to take Oscar's hand. As he did so, Oscar noticed a tiny blob of blue jelly in Grandad's hair.

Grandad passed something into Oscar's

palm and whispered a single word into his ear.

'Pwned.'

He straightened up and winked.

Oscar stood there, confused. What on earth had Grandad meant?

It was only after he'd waved Grandad off and watched the car disappear down the road that Oscar opened his fist.

This time Grandad hadn't given him a boiled sweet.

He'd given him a ring.

The Ring of Gnir.

It all started with a Scarecrow.

Puffin is seventy years old.
Sounds ancient, doesn't it? But Puffin has never been so lively. We're always on the lookout for the next big idea, which is how it began all those years ago.

Penguin Books was a big idea from the mind of a man called Allen Lane, who in 1935 invented the quality paperback and changed the world.
And from great Penguins, great Puffins grew, changing the face of children's books forever.

The first four Puffin Picture Books were hatched in 1940 and the first Puffin story book featured a man with broomstick arms called Worzel Gummidge. In 1967 Kaye Webb, Puffin Editor, started the Puffin Club, promising to **'make children into readers'.** She kept that promise and over 200,000 children became devoted Puffineers through their quarterly instalments of *Puffin Post*, which is now back for a new generation.

Many years from now, we hope you'll look back and remember Puffin with a smile. **No matter what your age or what you're into, there's a Puffin for everyone.** The possibilities are endless, but one thing is for sure: whether it's a picture book or a paperback, a sticker book or a hardback, **if it's got that little Puffin on it – it's bound to be good.**